# HORRID HENRY

## AND THE
## ABOMINABLE SNOWMAN

# Meet HORRID HENRY
## the laugh-out-loud
## worldwide sensation!

........................................................................

* Over 15 million copies sold in 27 countries and counting

* # 1 chapter book series in the UK

* Francesca Simon is the only American author to ever win the Galaxy British Book Awards Children's Book of the year (past winners include J.K. Rowling, Philip Pullman, and Eoin Colfer).

## "will make you laugh out loud."
## —Sunday Times

"**Kids will love reading the laugh-out-loud funny stories** about someone whose behavior is even worse than their own." —*School Library Journal*

"Humor is a proven enticement for reluctant readers, and **Francesca Simon's Horrid Henry series locates the funny bone with ease.**" —*Newsday*

"**What is brilliant about the books is that Henry never does anything that is subversive**. She creates an aura of supreme naughtiness (of which children are in awe) but points out that he operates within a safe and secure world...**eminently readable** books." —Emily Turner, *Angels and Urchins*

"**Kids who love funny books will love the Horrid Henry series** by Francesca Simon...Simon's hilariously dead-pan text is wonderfully complemented by Tony Ross's illustrations, which comically capture the consequences of Henry's horridness." —*Scripps Howard News Service*

"Accompanied by fantastic black-and-white drawings, the book is a joy to read. **Horrid Henry has an irresistible appeal to everyone—child and adult alike!** He is the child everyone is familiar with—irritating, annoying, but you still cannot help laughing when he gets into yet another scrape. Not quite a devil in disguise but you cannot help wondering at times! No wonder he is so popular!" —Angela Youngman

## Horrid Henry by Francesca Simon

Horrid Henry

Horrid Henry Tricks the Tooth Fairy

Horrid Henry and the Mega-Mean Time Machine

Horrid Henry's Stinkbomb

Horrid Henry and the Mummy's Curse

Horrid Henry and the Soccer Fiend

Horrid Henry's Underpants

Horrid Henry and the Scary Sitter

Horrid Henry's Christmas

Horrid Henry and the Abominable Snowman

Horrid Henry's Joke Book

# HORRID HENRY

## AND THE
## ABOMINABLE SNOWMAN

Francesca Simon
*Illustrated by* Tony Ross

sourcebooks
jabberwocky

Text © Francesca Simon 2007
Internal illustrations © Tony Ross 2007
Cover illustration © Tony Ross 2008
Cover and internal design © 2010 by Sourcebooks, Inc.

Published by Sourcebooks Jabberwocky, an imprint of Sourcebooks, Inc.
P.O. Box 4410, Naperville, Illinois 60567-4410
(630) 961-3900
Fax: (630) 961-2168
www.jabberwockykids.com

Originally published in Great Britain in 2007 by Orion Children's Books.

Library of Congress Cataloging-in-Publication data is on file with the publisher.

Source of Production: Versa Press, East Peoria, Illinois, USA
Date of Production: July 2010
Run Number: 12933

Printed and bound in the United States of America.
VP 10 9 8 7 6 5 4 3 2 1

*For my niece, Ava Rose*

# CONTENTS

# 1

## HORRID HENRY AND THE ABOMINABLE SNOWMAN

Moody Margaret took aim.

Thwack!

A snowball whizzed past and smacked Sour Susan in the face.

"AAAAARRGGHHH!" shrieked Susan.

"Ha ha, got you," said Margaret.

"You big meanie," howled Susan, scooping up a fistful of snow and hurling it at Margaret.

Thwack!

Susan's snowball smacked Moody Margaret in the face.

"OWWWW!" screamed Margaret. "You've blinded me."

"Good!" screamed Susan.

"I hate you!" shouted Margaret, shoving Susan.

"I hate you more!" shouted Susan, pushing Margaret.

Splat! Margaret toppled into the snow.

Splat! Susan toppled into the snow.

"I'm going home to build my own snowman," sobbed Susan.

"Fine. I'll win without you," said Margaret.

"Will not!"

"Will too! I'm going to win, copycat," shrieked Margaret.

"*I'm* going to win," shrieked Susan. "I kept my best ideas secret."

"Win? Win what?" demanded Horrid Henry, stomping down his front steps in his snow boots and swaggering over. Henry could hear the word *win* from miles away.

"Haven't you heard about the

competition?" said Sour Susan. "The prize is—"

"Shut up! Don't tell him," shouted Moody Margaret, packing snow onto her snowman's head.

Win? Competition? Prize? Horrid Henry's ears quivered. What secret were they trying to keep from him? Well, not for long. Horrid Henry was an expert at extracting information.

"Oh, the competition. I know all

3

about *that*," lied Horrid Henry. "Hey, great snowman," he added, strolling casually over to Margaret's snowman and pretending to admire her work.

Now, what should he do? Torture? Margaret's ponytail was always a tempting target. And snow down her sweater would make her talk.

What about blackmail? He could spread some great rumors about Margaret at school. Or…

"Tell me about the competition or the ice guy gets it," said Horrid Henry suddenly, leaping over to the snowman and putting his hands around its neck.

"You wouldn't dare," gasped Moody Margaret.

Henry's mittened hands got ready to push.

"Bye bye, head," hissed Horrid Henry. "Nice knowing you."

Margaret's snowman wobbled.

"Stop!" screamed Margaret. "I'll tell you. It doesn't matter 'cause you'll never ever win."

"Keep talking," said Horrid Henry warily, watching out in case Susan tried to ambush him from behind.

"Frosty Freeze is having a best snowman competition," said Moody Margaret, glaring. "The winner gets a year's free supply of ice cream. The judges will decide tomorrow morning. Now get away from my snowman."

Horrid Henry walked off in a daze, his jaw dropping. Margaret and Susan pelted him with snowballs but Henry didn't even notice. Free ice cream for a year direct from the Frosty Freeze Ice Cream factory. Oh wow! Horrid Henry couldn't believe it. Mom and Dad were so mean and horrible they hardly ever let him have ice cream. And when they did, they never *ever* let him put on his own hot fudge sauce and whipped cream and sprinkles. Or even scoop the ice cream himself. Oh no.

Well, when he won the Best Snowman Competition they couldn't stop him from gorging on Chunky Chocolate Fab Fudge Caramel Delight or Vanilla Whip Tutti-Frutti Toffee Treat. Oh boy! Henry could taste that glorious ice cream now. He'd live on ice cream. He'd bathe in ice cream. He'd sleep in ice cream. Everyone from school would turn up at his house when the Frosty Freeze truck arrived bringing his weekly barrels. No matter how much they begged, Horrid Henry would send them all away. No way was he sharing a drop of his precious ice cream with *anyone*.

And all he had to do was build the best snowman in the neighborhood. Pah! Henry's was sure to be the winner. He would build the biggest snowman of all. And not just a snowman. A snowman with claws and horns and fangs. A vampire-demon-monster snowman. An Abominable Snowman. Yes!

Henry watched Margaret and Susan rolling snow and packing their saggy snowman. Ha. Snow heap, more like.

"You'll never win with *that*," jeered Horrid Henry. "Your snowman is pathetic."

"Better than yours," snapped Margaret. Horrid Henry rolled his eyes.

"Obviously, because I haven't started mine yet."

"We've got a big head start on you, so ha ha ha," said Susan. "We're building a ballerina snowgirl."

"Shut up, Susan," screamed Margaret.

A ballerina snowgirl? What a stupid idea. If that was the best they could do, Henry was sure to win.

"Mine will be the biggest, the best, the most gigantic snowman ever seen," said Horrid Henry. "And much better than your stupid snow dwarf."

"Fat chance," sneered Margaret.

"Yeah, Henry," sneered Susan. "Ours is the best."

"No way," said Horrid Henry, starting to roll a gigantic ball of snow for Abominable's big belly. There was no time to lose.

Up the path, down the path, across the garden, down the side, back and forth, back and forth, Horrid Henry rolled the biggest ball of snow ever seen.

"Henry, can I build a snowman with you?" came a little voice.

"No," said Henry, starting to carve out some clawed feet.

"Oh please," said Peter. "We could build a great big one together. Like a bunny snowman, or a—"

"No!" said Henry. "It's *my* snowman. Build your own."

"Moooommmm!" wailed Peter. "Henry won't let me build a snowman with him."

"Don't be horrid, Henry," said Mom. "Why don't you build one together?"

"NO!!!" said Horrid Henry. He wanted to make his *own* snowman.

If he built a snowman with his stupid worm brother, he'd have to share the prize. Well, no way. He wanted all that ice cream for himself. And his Abominable Snowman was sure to be the best. Why share a prize when you didn't have to?

"Get away from my snowman, Peter," hissed Henry.

Perfect Peter sniveled. Then he started to roll a tiny ball of snow.

"And get your own snow," said Henry. "All this is mine."

"Mooooom!" wailed Peter. "Henry's hogging all the snow."

"We're done," trilled Moody Margaret. "Beat *this* if you can."

Horrid Henry looked at Margaret and Susan's snowgirl, complete with a big pink tutu wound around the waist. It was as big as Margaret.

"That old heap of snow is nothing compared to *mine*," bragged Horrid Henry.

Moody Margaret and Sour Susan looked at Henry's Abominable Snowman, complete with horned Viking helmet, fangs, and hairy scary claws. It was a few inches taller than Henry.

"Nah nah ne nah nah, mine's bigger," boasted Henry.

"Nah nah ne nah nah, mine's better," boasted Margaret.

"How do you like *my* snowman?" said Peter. "Do you think *I* could win?"

Horrid Henry stared at Perfect Peter's tiny snowman. It didn't even have a head, just a long, thin, lumpy body with two stones stuck in the top for eyes.

Horrid Henry howled with laughter.

"That's the worst snowman I've ever seen," said Henry. "It doesn't even have a head. That's a snow carrot."

"It is not," wailed Peter. "It's a big bunny."

"Henry! Peter! Dinner time," called Mom.

Henry stuck out his tongue at Margaret.

"And don't you dare touch my snowman."

Margaret stuck out her tongue at Henry.

"And don't you dare touch *my* snowgirl."

"I'll be watching you, Margaret."

"I'll be watching *you*, Henry."

They glared at each other.

★ ★ ★

Henry woke.

What was that noise? Was Margaret sabotaging his snowman? Was Susan stealing his snow?

Horrid Henry dashed to the window.

Phew. There was his Abominable Snowman, big as ever, dwarfing every other snowman on the street. Henry's was definitely the biggest, and the best. Mmm boy, he could taste that Triple Fudge Gooey Chocolate Chip Peanut Butter Marshmallow Custard ice cream right now.

Horrid Henry climbed back into bed.

A tiny doubt nagged him.

Was his snowman *definitely* bigger than Margaret's?

'Course it was, thought Henry.

"Are you sure?" rumbled his tummy.

"Yeah," said Henry.

"Because I really want that ice cream," growled his tummy. "Why don't you double-check?"

Horrid Henry got out of bed.

He was sure his was bigger and better than Margaret's. He was absolutely sure his was bigger and better.

But what if—

I can't sleep without checking, thought Henry.

Tip toe.

Tip toe.

Tip toe.

Horrid Henry slipped out of the front door.

The whole street was silent and white and frosty. Every house had a snowman in front. All of them much smaller than Henry's, he noted with satisfaction.

And there was his Abominable Snowman looming up, Viking horns scraping the sky. Horrid Henry gazed at him proudly. Next to him was Peter's pathetic pimple, with its stupid black stones. A snow lump, thought Henry.

Then he looked over at Margaret's snowgirl. Maybe it had fallen down, thought Henry hopefully. And if it hadn't, maybe he could help it on its way...

He looked again. And again. That evil fiend!

Margaret had sneaked an extra ball of snow on top, complete with a huge flowery hat.

That little cheater, thought Horrid Henry indignantly. She'd sneaked out after bedtime and made hers bigger than his. How dare she? Well, he'd fix Margaret. He'd add more snow to his right away.

Horrid Henry looked around. Where could he find more snow? He'd already used up every drop on his front lawn to build his giant, and no new snow had fallen.

Henry shivered.

Brr, it was freezing. He needed more snow, and he needed it fast. His slippers were starting to feel very wet and cold.

Horrid Henry eyed Peter's pathetic lump of snow. Hmmm, thought Horrid Henry.

Hmmm, thought Horrid Henry again.

Well, it's not doing any good sitting

there, thought Henry. Someone could trip over it. Someone could hurt himself. In fact, Peter's snow lump was a danger. He had to act fast before someone fell over it and broke a leg.

Quickly, he scooped up Peter's

snowman and stacked it carefully on top of his. Then, standing on his tippy-toes, he balanced the Abominable Snowman's Viking horns on top.

Ta-da!

Much better. And *much* bigger than Margaret's.

Teeth chattering, Horrid Henry sneaked back into his house and crept into bed. Ice cream, here I come, thought Horrid Henry.

Ding dong.

Horrid Henry jumped out of bed. What a morning to oversleep.

Perfect Peter ran and opened the door.

"We're from the Frosty Freeze Ice Cream Factory," said the man, beaming. "And you've got the winning snowman out front."

"I won!" screeched Horrid Henry. "I won!" He tore down the stairs and out the door. Oh what a wonderful, wonderful day. The sky was blue. The sun was shining—huh???

Horrid Henry looked around.

Horrid Henry's Abominable Snowman was gone.

"Margaret!" screamed Henry. "I'll kill you!"

But Moody Margaret's snowgirl was gone too.

The Abominable Snowman's helmet lay on its side on the ground. All that was left of Henry's snowman was... Peter's pimple, with its two black stone

eyes. A big blue ribbon was pinned to the top.

"But that's *my* snowman," said Perfect Peter.

"But…but…" said Horrid Henry.

"You mean, *I* won?" said Peter.

"That's wonderful, Peter," said Mom.

"That's fantastic, Peter," said Dad.

"All the others melted," said the Frosty Freeze man. "Yours was the only one left. It must have been a giant."

"It was," howled Horrid Henry.

# 2

## HORRID HENRY'S RAINY DAY

Horrid Henry was bored. Horrid Henry was fed up. He'd been banned from the computer for rampaging through Our Town Museum. He'd been banned from watching TV just because he was caught watching a *teeny* tiny bit extra after he'd been told to switch it off right after Mutant Max. Could he help it if an exciting new series about a rebel robot had started right after? How would he know if it were any good unless he watched some of it?

It was completely unfair and all Peter's fault for telling on him, and Mom and

Dad were the meanest, most horrible parents in the world.

And now he was stuck indoors, all day long, with absolutely nothing to do.

The rain splattered down. The house was gray. The world was gray. The universe was gray.

"I'm bored!" wailed Horrid Henry.

"Read a book," said Mom.

"Do your homework," said Dad.

"NO!" said Horrid Henry.

"Then tidy your room," said Mom.

"Unload the dishwasher," said Dad.

"Empty the garbage," said Mom.

"NO WAY!" shrieked Horrid Henry. What was he, a slave? Better keep out of his parents' way or they'd come up with even more horrible things for him to do.

Horrid Henry stomped up to his boring bedroom and slammed the door. Uggh. He hated all his toys. He hated all his music. He hated all his games.

UGGGHHHHHH! What could he do? Aha.

He could always check to see what Peter was up to.

Perfect Peter was sitting in his room arranging stamps in his stamp album.

"Peter is a baby, Peter is a baby," jeered Horrid Henry, sticking his head around the door.

"Don't call me baby," said Perfect Peter.

"OK, duke of poop," said Henry.

"Don't call me duke!" shrieked Peter.

"OK, poopsicle," said Henry.

"MOOOOM!" wailed Peter. "Henry called me poopsicle!"

"Don't be horrid, Henry!" shouted Mom. "Stop calling your brother names."

Horrid Henry smiled sweetly at Peter.

"OK, Peter, 'cause I'm so nice, I'll let you make a list of ten names that you don't want to be called," said Henry. "And it will only cost you $1."

A dollar! Perfect Peter could not believe his ears. Peter would pay much more than that never to be called poopsicle again.

"Is this a trick, Henry?" said Peter.

"No," said Henry. "How dare you? I make you a good offer, and you accuse me. Well, just for that—"

"Wait," said Peter. "I accept." He handed Henry a dollar bill. At last, all those horrid names would be banned. Henry would never call him duke of poop again.

Peter got out a piece of paper and a pencil.

Now, let's see, what to put on the list, thought Peter. Poopsicle, for a start. And I hate being called baby and diaper face and duke of poop. Peter wrote and wrote and wrote.

"OK, Henry, here's the list," said Peter.

## NAMES I DON'T WANT TO BE CALLED

1. Poopsicle
2. Duke of Poop
3. Ugly
4. Diaperface
5. Baby
6. Toad
7. Smelly toad
8. Ugg
9. Worm
10. Potty pants

Horrid Henry scanned the list. "Fine, stinky pants," said Henry. "Sorry, I meant poopy pants. Or was it smelly diaper?"

"MOOOMM!" wailed Peter. "Henry's calling me names!"

"Henry!" screamed Mom. "For the last time, can't you leave your brother alone?"

Horrid Henry considered. *Could* he leave that worm alone?

"Peter is a frog, Peter is a frog," chanted Henry.

"MOOOOOOMMMMM!" screamed Peter.

"That's it, Henry!" shouted Mom. "No allowance for a week. Go to your room and stay there."

"Fine!" shrieked Henry. "You'll all be sorry when I'm dead." He stomped down the hall and slammed his bedroom door as hard as he could. *Why* were his parents so mean and horrible? He was hardly bothering Peter at all. Peter *was* a frog. Henry was only telling the truth.

Boy would they be sorry when he'd died of boredom stuck up here.

If only we'd let him watch a little extra

TV, Mom would wail. Would
that have been so terrible?

If only we hadn't made
him do any chores, Dad
would sob.

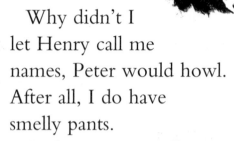

Why didn't I
let Henry call me
names, Peter would howl.
After all, I do have
smelly pants.

And now
it's too late and we're
sooooooo sorry, they
would shriek.

But wait. *Would* they be
sorry? Peter would grab his room. And
all his best toys. His archenemy Stuck-
Up Steve could come over and snatch
anything he wanted, even his skeleton
bank and Goo-Shooter. Peter could
invade the Purple Hand fort and Henry
couldn't stop him. Moody Margaret

could hop over the wall and steal his flag. And his cookies. And his Dungeon Drink Kit. Even his…Waterblaster.

NOOOOOO!!!

Horrid Henry went pale. He had to stop those greedy thieves. But how?

I could come back and haunt them, thought Horrid Henry. Yes! That would teach those grave robbers not to mess with me.

"OOOOOOO, get out of my rooooooooooom, you horrrrrrrrible tooooooooooooad," he would moan at Peter.

"Touch my Goooooooo-shoooooter and you'll be morphed into ectoplasm," he'd groan spookily from under Stuck-Up Steve's bed. Ha! That would show him.

Or he'd pop out from inside Moody Margaret's closet.

"Giiiiive Henrrrrry's toyyyys back, you mis-er-a-ble sliiiiiimy snake," he would rasp. That would teach her a thing or two.

Henry smiled. But fun as it would be to haunt people, he'd rather stop

horrible enemies from snatching his stuff
in the first place.

And then suddenly Horrid Henry had
a brilliant, spectacular idea. Hadn't Mom
told him just the other day that people
wrote wills to say who they wanted to
get all their stuff when they died? Henry
had been thrilled.

"So when you die I get all your
money!" Henry beamed.
Wow. The house
would be his! And
the car! And he'd be
boss of the TV, 'cause
it would be his too!!!
And the only shame was—

"Couldn't you just give it all to me
now?" asked Henry.

"Henry!" snapped Mom. "Don't be
horrid."

There was no time to lose. He had to
write a will immediately.

Horrid Henry sat down at his desk and grabbed some paper.

## MY WILL
## WARNING: DO NOT READ UNLESS
## I AM DEAD!!!! I mean it!!!!

If you're reading this it's because I'm dead and you aren't. I wish you were dead and I wasn't, so I could have all *your* stuff. It's so not fair.

First of all, to anyone thinking of stealing my stuff just 'cause I'm dead...BEWARE! Anyone who doesn't do what I say will get haunted by a bloodless and boneless ghoul, namely me. So there.

Now the hard part, thought Horrid Henry. Who should get his things? Was anyone deserving enough?

**Peter, you are a worm. And a toad. And an ugly baby diaper face smelly ugg potty pants poopsicle. I leave you...**hmmmm. That toad really shouldn't get anything. But Peter was his brother after all. **I leave you my candy wrappers. And a muddy twig.**

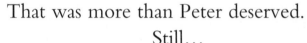

That was more than Peter deserved.

Still…

**Steve, you are stuck-up and horrible and the world's worst cousin. You can have a pair of my socks. You can choose the blue ones with the holes or the falling down orange ones.**

**Margaret, you nit-face. I give you the Purple Hand flag to remember me by— NOT! You can have two radishes and the knight**

with the chopped-off head.
And keep your paws off
my Grisly Grub Box!!!
Or else...

Miss Battle-Axe,
you are my worst
teacher ever. I leave
you a broken pencil.

Aunt Ruby, you can
have the lime

green cardigan back that
you gave me for Christmas.

Hmmm. So far he
wasn't doing so well giving
away any of his good things.

Ralph, you can have my Goo-Shooter, but
ONLY if you give *me* your football and your
bike and your computer game Slime Ghouls.

That was more like it. After all, why
should *he* be the only one writing a will?
It was certainly a lot more fun thinking

about *getting* stuff from other people than giving away his own treasures.

In fact, wouldn't he be better off helping others by telling them what he wanted? Wouldn't it be awful if Rich Aunt Ruby left him some of Steve's old clothes in her will thinking that he would be delighted? Better write to her at once.

Dear Aunt Ruby
I am leeving you
Something ~~grat REELY~~
~~GREAT~~ REELY
REELY GREAT in
my will, so make sure
you leeve me loads of
Cash in yours.
Your favorite nephew
Henry

Now, Steve. Henry was leaving him an old pair of holey socks. But Steve didn't have to *know* that, did he? For all Henry knew, Steve *loved* holey socks.

> Dear Steve
>
> You know your new blue racing bike with the silver trim? Well when your dead it wont be any use to you, So please leave it to me in your will
>
> Your favourite cousin
> Henry
>
> P.S By the way, No need to wait till your dead, you can give it to me now.

Right, Mom and Dad. When they were in the old people's home they'd

hardly need a thing. A rocking chair and
blanket each would do fine for them.

So, how would Dad's music system
look in his bedroom? And where could
he put Mom's clock radio? Henry had
always liked the chiming clock on their
mantelpiece and the picture of the
blackbird. Better go and check to see
where he could put them.

Henry went into Mom and Dad's
room and grabbed an armload of stuff.

He staggered to his bedroom and dumped everything on the floor, then went back for a second helping.

Stumbling and staggering under his heavy burden, Horrid Henry swayed down the hall and crashed into Dad.

"What are you doing?" said Dad, staring. "That's mine."

"And those are mine," said Mom.

"What is going on?" shrieked Mom and Dad.

"I was just checking how all this stuff will look in my room when you're in the old people's home," said Horrid Henry.

"I'm not there yet," said Mom.

"Put everything back," said Dad.

Horrid Henry scowled. Here he was, just trying to think ahead, and he gets told off.

"Well, just for that I won't leave you any of my knights in my will," said Henry.

Honestly, some people were so selfish.

# 3

# MOODY MARGARET'S MAKEOVER

"Watch out, Gurinder! You're smearing your nail polish," screeched Moody Margaret. "Violet! Don't touch your face—you're spoiling all my hard work. Susan! Sit still."

"I am sitting still," said Sour Susan. "Stop pulling my hair."

"I'm not pulling your hair," hissed Margaret. "I'm styling it."

"Ouch!" squealed Susan. "You're hurting me."

"I am not, crybaby."

"I'm not a crybaby," howled Susan. Moody Margaret sighed loudly.

"Not everyone can be naturally beautiful like me. Some people"—she glared at Susan—"have to work at it."

"You're not beautiful," said Sour Susan, snorting.

"I am too," said Margaret, primping herself.

"Are not," said Susan. "On the ugly scale of 1 to 10, with 1 being the ugliest, wartiest toad, you're a 2."

"Huh!" said Margaret. "Well, *you're* so ugly you're minus 1. They don't have an ugly enough scale for *you*."

"I want my money back!" shrieked Susan.

"No way!" shrieked Margaret. "Now sit down and shut up."

Across the wall in the next garden, deep inside the branches hiding the top secret entrance of the Purple Hand fort, a master spy pricked up his ears.

*Money?* Had he heard the word *money?*

What was going on next door?

Horrid Henry zipped out of his fort and dashed to the low wall separating his yard from Margaret's. Then he stared. And stared some more. He'd seen many weird things in his life. But nothing as weird as this.

Moody Margaret, Sour Susan, Lazy Linda, Vain Violet, and Gorgeous Gurinder were sitting in Margaret's garden. Susan had rollers tangling her pink hair. Violet had blue mascara all over her face. Linda was covered in gold glitter. There was spilled nail polish, face powder, and broken lipstick all over Margaret's patio.

Horrid Henry burst out laughing.

"Are you playing clowns?" said Henry.

"Huh, shows how much *you* know, Henry," said Margaret. "*I'm* doing makeovers."

"What's that?" said Henry.

"It's when you change how people look, dummy," said Margaret.

"I knew that," lied Henry. "I just wanted to see if you did."

Margaret waved a flyer in his face.

# MARGARET'S
## MAGNIFICENT MAKEOVERS!

I can make *you* beautiful!
Yes, even YOU.
No one too old or too ugly.
Only $1 for a new you!!!!!
# Hurry!
Special offer ends soon!!!!!!!!!!!

Makeovers? Makeovers? What an incredibly stupid idea. Who'd pay to have a moody old grouch like Margaret smear gunk all over their face? Ha! No one.

Horrid Henry started laughing and pointing.

Vain Violet looked like a demon with red and blue and purple gloop all over her face. Gorgeous Gurinder looked as if a paint pot had been poured down her

51

cheeks. Linda's hair looked as if she'd been struck by lightning.

But Violet wasn't screaming and yanking Margaret's hair out. Instead she handed Margaret—*money*.

"Thanks, Margaret, I look amazing," said Vain Violet, admiring herself in the mirror. Henry waited for the mirror to crack.

It didn't.

"Thanks, Margaret," said Gurinder. "I look so fantastic I hardly recognize myself." And she also handed Margaret a dollar.

Two whole dollars? Were they mad?

"Are you getting ready for the Monster's Ball?" jeered Henry.

"Shut up, Henry," said Vain Violet.

"Shut up, Henry," said Gorgeous Gurinder.

"You're just jealous because I'm going to be rich and you're not," said Margaret. "Nah nah ne nah nah."

"Why don't we give Henry a makeover?" said Violet.

"Good idea," said Moody Margaret. "He could sure use one."

"Yeah," said Sour Susan.

Horrid Henry took a step back.

Margaret advanced toward him wielding nail polish and a hairbrush. Violet followed clutching a lipstick, hair dye, and other instruments of torture.

Yikes! Horrid Henry dashed back to the safety of his fort as fast as he could, trying to ignore the horrible, cackling laughter.

He sat on his Purple Hand throne and scarfed some extra tasty chocolate cookies from the secret stash he'd swiped from Margaret yesterday. Makeovers! Ha! How dumb could you get? Trust a pea-brained grouch like Margaret to come up with such a stupid idea. Who in their right mind would want a makeover?

On the other hand…

Horrid Henry had actually seen

Margaret being paid. And good money, too, just for smearing some colored gunk onto people's faces and yanking their hair around.

Hmmmm.

Horrid Henry started to think. Maybe Margaret *did* have a little eensy-weensy teeny-tiny bit of a good idea. And, naturally, anything she could do, Henry could do much, much better. Margaret obviously didn't know the first thing about makeovers, so why should *she* make all that money, thought Horrid Henry indignantly. He'd steal— no, *borrow*—her idea and do it better. Much much better. He'd make people look *really* fantastic.

Henry's Makeovers. Henry's Marvelous
Makeovers. Henry's Miraculous Makeovers.

He'd be rich! With some false teeth
and a red marker he could turn Miss
Battle-Axe into a vampire. Mrs. Oddbod
could be a perfect Dracula. And wouldn't
Stuck-Up Steve be improved after a short
visit from the Makeover Magician? Even
Aunt Ruby wouldn't recognize him
when Henry had finished. Tee-hee.

First, he needed supplies. That was
easy: Mom had tons of gunk for smearing
all over her face. And if he ran out he
could always use crayons and glue.

Horrid Henry dashed to the bathroom and helped himself to a few handfuls of Mom's makeup. What on earth did she need all this stuff for? thought Henry, piling it into a bag. About time someone cleared out this drawer. Then he wrote a few flyers.

Horrid Henry, Makeover Magician, was ready for business.

All he needed were some customers. Preferably rich, ugly customers. Now, where could he find some of those?

Henry strolled into the living room. Dad was reading on the sofa. Mom was working at the computer.

Horrid Henry looked at his aged, wrinkly, boring old parents. Bleeeccch!

Boy, could they be improved, thought

Henry. How could he tactfully persuade these potential customers that they needed his help—fast?

"Mom," said Henry, "you know Great-Aunt Greta?"

"Yes," said Mom.

"Well, you're starting to look just like her."

"What?" said Mom.

"Yup," said Horrid Henry, "old and ugly. Except—" he peered at her, "you have more wrinkles."

"*What?*" squeaked Mom.

"And Dad looks like a gargoyle," said Henry.

"Huh?" said Dad.

"Only scarier," said Henry. "But don't worry, I can help."

"Oh really?" said Mom.

"Oh really?" said Dad.

"Yeah," said Henry, "I'm doing makeovers." He handed Mom and Dad a flyer.

# Are you ugly?

Are you very very ugly?

Do you look like the creature from the black lagoon? (Only worse?)

Then today is your lucky day!

# HENRY'S
# MARVELOUS MAKEOVERS.

Only $2 for an exciting new you!!!!!!

"So, how many makeovers would you like?" said Horrid Henry. "Ten? Twenty? Maybe more 'cause you're so old and need a lot of work to fix you."

"Make over someone else," said Mom, scowling.

"Make over someone else," said Dad, scowling.

Boy, talk about ungrateful, thought Horrid Henry.

"Me first!"

"No me!"

Screams were coming from Margaret's garden. Kung-Fu Kate and Singing Soraya were about to become her latest victims. Well, not if Henry could help it.

"Step right up, get your makeovers here!" shouted Henry. "Miracle Makeovers, from an expert. Only $2 for a brand-new you."

"Leave my customers alone, copycat!"

hissed Moody Margaret, holding out her
hand to snatch Kate's dollar.

Henry ignored her.

"You look boring, Kate," said Henry.
"Why don't you let a *real* expert give
you a makeover?"

"You?" said Kate.

"Two dollars and you'll look
completely different," said Horrid
Henry. "Guaranteed."

"Margaret's only charging $1," said Kate.

"My special offer today is 75 cents for

the first makeover," said Henry quickly. "And free beauty advice," he added.

Soraya looked up. Kate stood up from Margaret's chair.

"Such as?" scowled Margaret. "Go on, tell us."

Eeeek. What on earth *was* a beauty tip? If your face is dirty, wash it? Use a lice comb? Horrid Henry had no idea.

"Well, in your case, wear a bag over your head," said Horrid Henry. "Or a bucket."

Susan snickered.

"Ha ha, very funny," snapped Margaret. "Come on, Kate. Don't let him trick you. *I'm* the makeover expert."

"I'm going to try Henry," said Kate.

"Me too," said Soraya.

Yippee! His first customers. Henry stuck out his tongue at Margaret.

Kung-Fu Kate and Singing Soraya climbed over the wall and sat down on the bench at the picnic table. Henry opened his makeover bag and got to work.

"No peeking," said Henry. "I want you to be surprised."

Henry smeared and coated, primped and colored, slopped and glopped. This was easy!

"I'm so beautiful—hoo hoo hoo," hummed Soraya.

"Aren't you going to do my hair?" said Kung-Fu Kate.

"Of course," said Horrid Henry.

He emptied a bottle of glue on her head and scrunched it around.

"What did you put in?" said Kate.

"Secret hair potion," said Henry.

"What about *me?*" said Soraya.

"No problem," said Henry, shoveling in some red paint.

A bit of black here, a few blobs of red there, a smear of purple and...ta-da!

Henry stood back to admire his handiwork. Wow! Kung-Fu Kate looked *completely* different. So did Singing Soraya. Next time he'd charge $10. The moment people saw them everyone would want one of Henry's marvelous makeovers.

"You look amazing," said Horrid Henry. He had no idea he was such an awesome makeover artist. Customers would be lining up for his services. He'd need a bigger piggy bank.

"There, just like the Mummy,

Frankenstein, *and* a vampire," said Henry, handing Kate a mirror.

## "AAAARRRRGGGGHHH!"

screamed Kung-Fu Kate.

Soraya snatched the mirror.

## "AAAARRRRGGGGHHH!"

screamed Singing Soraya.

Horrid Henry stared at them. Honestly, there was no pleasing some people.

## "NOOOooooooo!"

squealed Kung-Fu Kate.

"But I thought you wanted to look amazing," said Henry.

"Amazingly good! Not scary!" wailed Kate.

"Has anyone seen my new lipsticks?" said Mom. "I could have sworn I put them in the—"

She caught sight of Soraya and Kate.

# "AAAAAAARRRRRGGGGGHHHH!"

screeched Mom. "Henry! How could you be so horrid? Go to your room."

"But…but…" gasped Horrid Henry. It was so unfair. Was it his fault his stupid customers didn't know when they looked great?

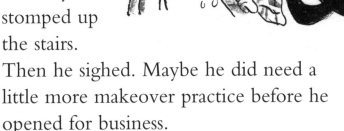

Henry stomped up the stairs.
Then he sighed. Maybe he did need a little more makeover practice before he opened for business.

Now, where could he find someone to practice on?

"I got an A on my spelling test," said Perfect Peter.

"I got a gold star for having the tidiest desk," said Tidy Ted.

"And I got in the Good as Gold book again," said Goody-Goody Gordon.

Henry burst into Peter's bedroom.

"I'm doing makeovers," said Horrid Henry. "Who wants to go first?"

"Ummm," said Peter.

"Ummm," said Ted.

"We're going to Sam's birthday party today," said Gordon.

"Even better," said Henry beaming. "I can make you look great for the party. Who's first?"

# 4

# HORRID HENRY'S AUTHOR VISIT

Horrid Henry woke up. He felt strange. He felt…happy. He felt…excited. But why?

Was it the weekend? No. Was it a day off school? No. Had Miss Battle-Axe been kidnapped by aliens and transported to another galaxy to slave in the salt mines? No (unfortunately).

So why was he feeling so excited on a school day?

And then Horrid Henry remembered.

Oh wow!! It was Book Week at Henry's school, and his favorite author in the whole world, TJ Fizz, the writer of the stupendous *Ghost Quest* and *Mad Machines* and *Skeleton Skunks*, was coming to talk to his class. Henry had read every single one of TJ's brilliant books, even after lights out. Rude Ralph thought they were almost as good as Mutant Max comics. Horrid Henry thought they were even better.

Perfect Peter bounced into his room.

"Isn't it exciting, Henry?" said Perfect Peter. "Our class is going to meet a real live author! Milksop Miles is coming today. He's the man who wrote *The Happy Nappy*. Do you think he'll sign my copy?"

Horrid Henry snorted.

*The Happy Nappy*! Only the dumbest book ever. All those giant diapers with names like Rappy Nappy and Zappy Nappy and Tappy Nappy dancing and prancing around. And then the truly horrible Gappy Nappy, who was always wailing, "I'm leaking!"

Horrid Henry shuddered. He was amazed that Milksop Miles dared to show his face after writing such a boring book.

"Only a wormy toad like you could like such a stupid story," said Henry.

"It's not stupid," said Peter.

"Is too."

"Is not. And he's bringing his guitar. Miss Lovely said so."

"Big deal," said Horrid Henry. "*We've* got TJ Fizz."

Perfect Peter shuddered.

"Her books are too scary," said Peter.

"That's 'cause you're a baby."

"Mom!" shrieked Peter. "Henry called me baby."

"Tattletale," hissed Henry.

"Don't be horrid, Henry," shouted Mom.

Horrid Henry sat in class with a huge tote bag filled with all his TJ Fizz books. Everyone in the class had drawn book covers for *Ghost Quest* and *Ghouls' Jewels,* and written their own *Skeleton Skunk* story. Henry's of course was the best: *Skeleton Skunk Meets*

*Terminator Gladiator: May the Smelliest Fighter Win!* He would give it to TJ Fizz if she paid him a million dollars.

Ten minutes to go. How could he live until it was time for her to arrive?

Miss Battle-Axe cleared her throat.

"Class, we have a very important guest coming. I know you're all very excited, but I will not tolerate anything but perfect behavior today. Anyone who misbehaves will be sent out. Is that clear?" She glared at Henry.

Henry scowled back. Of course he would be perfect. TJ Fizz was coming!

"Has everyone thought of a good question to ask her? I'll write the best ones on the board," continued Miss Battle-Axe.

"How much money do you make?" shouted Rude Ralph.

"How many TVs do you have?" shouted Horrid Henry.

"Do you like fudge?" shouted Greedy Graham.

"I said *good* questions," snapped Miss Battle-Axe. "Bert, what's your question for TJ Fizz?"

"I dunno," said Beefy Bert.

Rumble.

Rumble.

Rumble.

Ooops. Henry's tummy was telling him it was snack time.

It must be all the excitement. It was strictly forbidden to eat in class, but Henry was a master sneaker. He certainly wouldn't want his tummy to gurgle while TJ Fizz was talking.

Miss Battle-Axe was writing down Clever Clare's eight questions on the board.

Slowly, carefully, silently, Horrid Henry opened his lunch box under the table. Slowly, carefully, silently, he eased open the bag of chips.

Horrid Henry looked to the left.

Rude Ralph was waving his hand in the air.

Horrid Henry looked to the right.

Greedy Graham was drooling and opening a bag of candy.

The coast was clear. Henry popped some Super Spicy Hedgehog chips into his mouth.

MUNCH! CRUNCH!

"C'mon Henry, give me some chips," whispered Rude Ralph.

"No," hissed Horrid Henry. "Eat your own."

"I'm starving," moaned Greedy Graham. "Gimme a chip."

"No!" hissed Horrid Henry.

MUNCH CRUNCH! YANK

Huh?

Miss Battle-Axe towered over him, holding his bag of chips in the air. Her red eyes were like two icy daggers.

"What did I tell you, Henry?" said Miss Battle-Axe. "No bad behavior would be tolerated. Go to Miss Lovely's class."

"But…but…TJ Fizz is coming!" spluttered Horrid Henry. "I was just—"

Miss Battle-Axe pointed to the door. "Out!"

"NOOOOOOOOOO!" howled Henry.

Horrid Henry sat in a tiny chair at the back of Miss Lovely's room. Never had he suffered such torment. He tried to block his ears as Milksop Miles read his horrible book to Peter's class.

"Hello, Happy, Clappy, and Yappy! Can *you* find the leak?"

"No," said Happy.

"No," said Clappy.

"No," said Yappy.

"I can," said Gappy Nappy.

**AAAARRRRGGGGGHHH!** Horrid Henry gritted his teeth. He would go crazy having to listen to this a moment longer.

He had to get out of here.

"All together now, let's sing the 'Happy Nappy Song,'" trilled Milksop Miles, whipping out his guitar.

"Yay!" cheered the infants.

No, groaned Horrid Henry.

> Oh I'm a happy nappy,
> a happy zappy nappy
> I wrap up your bottom, snug and tight,
> And keep you dry all through the night
> Oh—

This was torture. No, this was worse than torture. How could he sit here listening to the horrible "Happy Nappy

Song" knowing that just above him
TJ Fizz was reading from one of her
incredible books, passing around the
famous skunk skeleton, and showing off
her *Ghost Quest* drawings? He had to get
back to his own class. He had to.

But how?

What if he joined in the singing? He
could bellow:

> Oh I'm a soggy nappy
> A smelly, stinky nappy—

Yes! That would certainly get him sent
out the door straight to—the principal.
Not back to his class and TJ Fizz.

Horrid Henry closed his mouth. Rats.

Maybe there'd be an earthquake? A
power failure? Where was a fire drill
when you needed one?

He could always pretend he needed to
use the restroom. But then when he didn't
come back, they'd come looking for him.

Or maybe he could just sneak away? Why not? Henry got to his feet and began to slide toward the door, trying to be invisible.

**Sneak** **Sneak** Sn—

"Whooa, come back here, little boy," shouted Milksop Miles, twanging his guitar. Henry froze. "Our party is just starting. Now who knows the Happy Nappy Dance?"

"I do," said Perfect Peter.

"I do," said Goody-Goody Gordon.

"We all do," said Tidy Ted.

"Everyone on their feet," said Milksop Miles. "Ah-one, ah-two, let's all do the Nappy Dance!"

"Nap nap nap nap nap nap nappy," warbled Miles.

"Nap nap nap nap nap nap nappy," warbled Peter's class, dancing away.

Desperate times call for desperate

81

measures. Horrid Henry started dancing. Slowly, he tapped his way closer and closer and closer to the door and—freedom!

Horrid Henry reached for the door knob. Miss Lovely was busy dancing in the corner. Just a few more steps…

"Who's going to be my little helper while we act out the story?" beamed Miles. "Who would like to play the Happy Nappy?"

"Me! Me!" squealed Miss Lovely's class.

Horrid Henry sank against the wall.

"Come on, don't be shy," said Miles, pointing straight at Henry. "Come on up and put on the magic happy nappy!" And he marched over and dangled an enormous blue diaper in front of Henry. It was over one yard wide and one yard high, with a hideous smiling face and big goggly eyes.

Horrid Henry took a step back. He

felt faint. The giant diaper was looming above him. In a moment it would be over his head and he'd be trapped inside. His name would be mud—forever. Henry the nappy. Henry the giant nappy. Henry the giant happy nappy…

"**AAAARRRRGGGGGHHH!**" screamed Horrid Henry. "Get away from me!"

Milksop Miles stopped waving the gigantic diaper.

"Oh dear," he said.

"Oh dear," said Miss Lovely.

"Don't be scared," said Miles.

Scared? Horrid Henry…scared? Of a giant diaper? Henry opened his mouth to scream.

And then he stopped.

What if…?

"Help! Help! I'm being attacked by a diaper!" screeched Henry. "HELLLLLLLP!"

Milksop Miles looked at Miss Lovely. Miss Lovely looked at Milksop Miles.

"HELLLLLLLP! HELLLLLLLP!"

"Henry? Are you OK?" piped Perfect Peter.

"NOOOOOOOOO!" wailed Horrid Henry, cowering. "I'm…I'm…diaper-phobic."

"Never mind," said Milksop Miles. "You're not the first boy who's been scared of a giant diaper."

"I'm sure I'll be fine if I go back to my own class," gasped Horrid Henry.

Miss Lovely hesitated. Horrid Henry opened his mouth to howl—

"Run along then," said Miss Lovely quickly.

Horrid Henry did not wait to be told twice.

He raced out of Miss Lovely's class, then dashed upstairs to his own.

*Skeleton Skunk* here I come, thought Henry, bursting through the door.

There was the great and glorious TJ

Fizz, just about to start reading a brand new chapter from her latest book, *Skeleton Stinkbomb*. Hallelujah, he was in time.

"Henry, what are you doing here?" hissed Miss Battle-Axe.

"Miss Lovely sent me back," beamed Horrid Henry. "And you did say we should be on our best behavior today, so I did what I was told."

Henry sat down as TJ began to read. The story was amazing.

Ahhh, sighed Horrid Henry happily, wasn't life grand?

The HORRiD HENRY books
by Francesca Simon

Illustrated by Tony Ross
*Each book contains four stories*

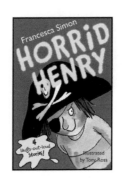

# HORRID HENRY

Henry is dragged to dancing class against his will; vies with Moody Margaret to make the yuckiest Glop; goes camping; and tries to be good like Perfect Peter—but not for long.

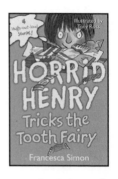

# HORRID HENRY TRICKS THE TOOTH FAIRY

Horrid Henry tries to trick the Tooth Fairy into giving him more money; sends Moody Margaret packing; causes his teachers to run screaming from school; and single-handedly wrecks a wedding.

## HORRID HENRY and THE MEGA-MEAN TIME MACHINE

Horrid Henry reluctantly goes for a hike; builds a time machine and convinces Perfect Peter that boys wear dresses in the future; Perfect Peter plays one of the worst tricks ever on his brother; and Henry's aunt takes the family to a fancy restaurant, so his parents bribe him to behave.

# HORRID HENRY'S
## STINKBOMB

Horrid Henry uses a
stinkbomb as a toxic weapon
in his long-running war
with Moody Margaret; uses all his tricks
to win the school reading competition;
goes for a sleepover and retreats in horror
when he finds that other people's houses
aren't always as nice as his own; and has
the joy of seeing Miss Battle-Axe in hot
water with the principle when he knows
it was all his fault.

# HORRID HENRY
# AND THE
# MUMMY'S CURSE

Horrid Henry indulges his favorite hobby— collecting Gizmos; has a bad time with his spelling homework; starts a rumor that there's a shark in the pool; and spooks Perfect Peter with the mummy's curse.

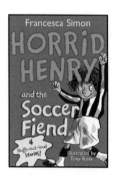

# HORRID HENRY
## AND THE
## SOCCER FIEND

Horrid Henry reads
Perfect Peter's diary and
improves it; goes shopping
with Mom and tries to make her buy
him some really nice new sneakers; is
horrified when his old enemy Bossy
Bill turns up at school; and tries by any
means, to win the class soccer match.

# HORRID HENRY'S UNDERPANTS

Horrid Henry discovers a genius way to write thank-you letters; negotiates over vegetables; competes with Perfect Peter over which of them is sickest; and finds himself wearing the wrong underpants—with dreadful consequences.

# HORRID HENRY
# AND THE
# SCARY SITTER

Horrid Henry encounters the worst babysitter in the world; traumatizes his parents on a long car trip; is banned from trick-or-treating at Halloween; and emerges victorious from a raid on Moody Margaret's Secret Club.

## HORRID HENRY'S CHRISTMAS

Four fabulously funny
stories that will invoke
every family's worst
Christmas nightmares,
as Horrid Henry sabotages the school
play; tries to do his Christmas shopping
without spending his allowance; attempts
to ambush Santa Claus (to get more
presents, of course); and endures the
worst Christmas dinner ever!

# HORRID HENRY'S JOKE BOOK

WARNING: Too rude for parents and for slimy toad little brothers!

These are Horrid Henry's very own jokes: the ones that grossed out Mom and Dad; that made Aunt Ruby run home; that sent Miss Battle-Axe screaming from class.

# About the Author

Photo: Francesco Guidicini

Francesca Simon spent her childhood on the beach in California and then went to Yale and Oxford Universities to study medieval history and literature. She now lives in London with her family. She has written over forty-five books and won the Children's Book of the Year in 2008 at the Galaxy British Book Awards for *Horrid Henry and the Abominable Snowman*.